SRJC
9/94

D0627126

A
FORTUNE
BRANCHES OUT

By Margaret Mahy:

Published by Delacorte Press

The Door in the Air and Other Stories

THE COUSINS QUARTET
The Good Fortunes Gang
A Fortunate Name
A Fortune Branches Out
Tangled Fortunes

BOOK THREE OF
THE COUSINS QUARTET

A FORTUNE BRANCHES OUT

MARGARET MAHY

ILLUSTRATED BY
MARIAN YOUNG

DELACORTE PRESS

Published by
Delacorte Press
Bantam Doubleday Dell Publishing Group, Inc.
1540 Broadway
New York, New York 10036

A Vanessa Hamilton Book

Book design by Claire Vaccaro

Library of Congress Cataloging in Publication Data
Mahy, Margaret.
A Fortune branches out / by Margaret Mahy ; illustrated by Marian Young.
p. cm. — (The Cousins quartet ; bk. 3)
Summary: Tessa Fortune and her cousins want to raise one hundred dollars for
the New Zealand National Telethon, but when their plans begin to go awry,
Tessa learns some valuable lessons about her goal of becoming a rich executive.
ISBN 0-385-32037-X
[1. Fund-raising—Fiction. 2. Moneymaking projects—Fiction. 3. Cousins—
Fiction. 4. New Zealand—Fiction.] I. Young, Marian, ill. II. Title. III. Series:
Mahy, Margaret. Cousins quartet ; bk. 3.
PZ7.M2773Fq 1994
[Fic]—dc20   93-11441
                                                                                             CIP
                                                                                             AC

Manufactured in the United States of America

April 1994

10   9   8   7   6   5   4   3   2   1

TO YVONNE, RON, KEN, JOAN,
JOYCE, AND ARTHUR—
MY COUSINS FROM NEXT DOOR

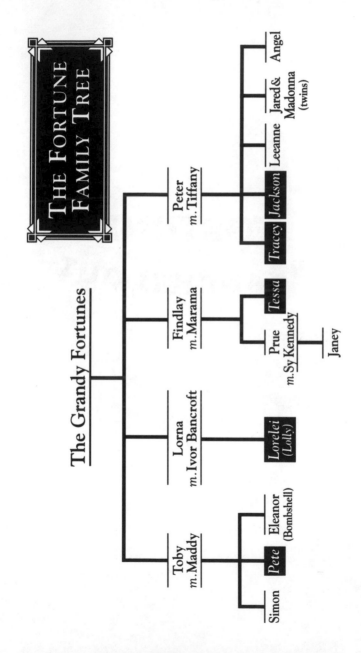

The Fortune Family Tree

The Grandy Fortunes

Toby *m.*Maddy
- Simon
- *Pete*
- Eleanor (Bombshell)

Lorna *m.*Ivor Bancroft
- *Lorelei (Lolly)*

Findlay *m.*Marama
- Prue *m.*Sy Kennedy
  - Janey
- *Tessa*

Peter *m.*Tiffany
- *Tracey*
- *Jackson*
- Leeanne
- Jared & Madonna (twins)
- Angel

CHAPTER 1

Tessa could never understand why people were so critical of her wish to become a rich corporate executive with a cellular phone. Nobody ever criticized Dick Whittington for setting out to seek his fortune. She was sure Dick Whittington would have enjoyed having a cellular phone as well as a cat.

"Tessa, don't expect to be paid for every single thing you do around the house," her mother, Marama, often said. "Money isn't everything, you know."

But if money wasn't everything, why did the world act as if it was? People *needed* it every day of their lives. "Money doesn't buy happiness," Marama had cried, shaking her head at Tessa.

"Yes, it does," Tessa cried, amazed that her

mother couldn't see this for herself. Television ads for lotteries and banks showed people being showered with money and looking radiantly happy. That was all Tessa wanted in life . . . to be radiantly happy and to have a cellular phone slung on her belt, just as the cowboy heroes in films about the Wild West carried their six-shooters. When she thought of her own savings nestling in the bank, Tessa felt something very *like* happiness. And, after all, she had *worked* to save it. She had washed cars, cleaned windows, cut lawns, and weeded gardens. Saving that money had been like an adventurous game in which she had pitted her wits against the world, and come out on top. So why shouldn't she enjoy the feeling?

"Other girls love horses and ballet," cried her mother despairingly. "Why don't you?" Tessa shrugged and wrinkled her forehead. Loving horses and ballet showed girls were warmhearted and artistic and if anybody loved making money, it meant that they were somehow horrible.

"Horses and ballet *cost* a lot," muttered Tessa now, standing under the tree at the Bright Street corner and looking proudly at the stand she had set up there. "Someone *pays* for them with money."

"Talking to yourself?" asked her cousin, Pete Fortune, from behind his armful of cardboard cartons. As Tessa turned to answer, a sound like a wolf howling swept toward her, then past her, and finally away from her.

"Yaaaaah! Fortune!" It was Grant Chilling, an old enemy, swinging dangerously around the Bright Street corner on his ten-speed bicycle.

"Dead-Loss Chilling," Pete said. "What an idiot! Okay! Let's get organized. First, we'll get the counter straight, and then we'll be in business, mate." Every now and then he talked in rhyme, though he never wrote poetry.

Tessa took out a thin book with a neatly folded slip of paper sticking out of it. The book was called *Succeed and Grow Rich* by Ellington Fillmore. Ellington Fillmore's photograph smiled from the back cover. *You, too, can climb the ladder of success,* he was saying in bold red print. The book was full of his wise sayings, and the back cover was filled with compliments from executive vice-presidents, all of whom owed their success to Ellington Fillmore's good advice. Tessa believed that if she followed Ellington's good advice she, too, might become an executive vice-president, with a high-rise office, a computer, a fax machine, and a laser printer. She might even become a president, telling mere vice-presidents how to do things. Tessa longed to succeed and grow rich.

This afternoon she was going to practice making

money, but nobody could call her greedy because the money she made would all be for other people. Tessa and her cousins, the members of the Good Fortunes Gang, were setting up a white elephant stand to raise money for the National Telethon's appeal on behalf of senior citizens.

Having put the cartons down on the counter under the Bright Street tree, Pete looked around curiously. "Where are the others?" he asked.

"Lorelei had to go home first and collect her white elephant cakes," Tessa said. "Tracey and Jackson said they'd come later. But they're not bringing anything. Tracey said her family eats every single thing in the house. There's never anything left over."

As a big truck lumbered down Main Road, a rush of diesel-smelling dust beat on Tessa's face and rustled the leaves over her head. She looked up into the tree. Sunshine dappled her face with warm patches. Tessa smiled. Her white elephant stand would look sunny and inviting to anyone still coming out of the Hamburgerama on the opposite corner. It would lure them closer. As she watched, a car drove by with a big sticker in its back window. SUPPORT NEW ZEALAND, it said. SUPPORT THE TELETHON. *That's just what I'm doing*, Tessa thought proudly.

The National Telethon took place every three years, always on behalf of some good cause or other. For twenty-four hours one particular television channel had no sports, no news, no cartoons, no advertisements, no miniseries, no quiz shows. Celebrities from overseas, rock singers, and stars of British or Australian soap operas worked for a night and a day in front of the cameras, joking, singing, laughing, and reading out messages, challenges, and promises of money phoned in by people. Large, important groups, like Air New Zealand, or small private family groups could take their contributions, big or little, to television studios. And while they stood there, handing over their money, cameras and lights would focus on them, and the soap opera stars would thank them and praise them for their kind hearts. Anyone could suddenly be a star. The Telethon was like a great money party sprawling across the whole country.

This year Tessa had decided to branch out on her own. *Organize people to organize themselves,* Ellington Fillmore advised. Tessa had organized the whole Fortune family—not only her cousins, but her uncles, aunts, and grandparents, as well—to bake cookies and donate jars of last year's jam. Her goal was to sell a hundred things at a dollar each. She imagined herself arriving at the Telethon center, specially set up in the Fairfield town hall, and saying carelessly,

"Here you are! A hundred dollars from the Fortune cousins." Then she would give a small speech about being kind to senior citizens. She had it written out and hidden in the back of *Succeed and Grow Rich*.

"Yaaaah! Fortune Finks!" howled Grant, cycling past again, but Tessa scarcely noticed him. She was too interested in arranging her white elephant wares . . . an old lamp, a lumpy china vase with handles like ears, a candlestick shaped like a banana, and several bottles of her grandmother's famous plum sauce. Tessa had also brought along an old adding machine she had found while spring-cleaning an office for her grandfather, but this was for adding up her profits. Her father had refused to lend her his calculator, even though it was only for the day. He said he needed it himself.

A shaggy-haired old man called Mr. Martello stopped and stared at Tessa and Pete as they worked on the stand.

"I hope you tidy all that away afterward, Tessa," he said severely. "It's a nice corner here. We don't want children playing shop and then leaving a lot of junk behind."

Playing shop! Tessa was insulted.

"It's a white elephant stand," she said. "We're raising money for the Telethon."

"Telethon! Telethon!" cried Mr. Martello in

tones of despair. "Where can I get away from it? Trampoline-athons! Rock-and-roll-athons! Are you part of the school sport-athon, then?"

"We're freelance," explained Tessa. "We're going to make a hundred dollars." (Just saying it made her feel as if she had made that magical amount of money already.) "It's for a good cause," she added, because that was what they were saying at school and on television too. *Support the Telethon. It's for such a good cause.* "It's to help senior citizens." *Like you,* she nearly added.

"Hmmmph!" said Mr. Martello. "All people talk about these days is money! I'm going to have my hair cut."

He turned in the direction of the Top Story Hair Salon. Tessa knew he was going to get *his* hair cut free, because his daughter-in-law worked at the Top Story Hair Salon. He would wait there, reading articles about Princess Di and Elizabeth Taylor in the hair salon magazines, and his daughter-in-law would clip him in between the rinses and hair sets of paying customers. It is easy to speak scornfully of money when you are on the way to get a free haircut, thought Tessa.

Mr. Martello stopped and looked back at her. It was as if he had suddenly tuned in to her thinking.

"Money isn't everything, you know," he said sternly.

"Yaaaah! Fortune!" shouted Grant Chilling, shooting past the tree once more. Ellington Fillmore had no good advice about what vice-presidents should do if people like Grant Chilling rode past their offices, shouting "Yaaaaah!" at them. *Have faith in yourself. Believe you are a winner and you will win*, he promised. *I* will *have faith in myself*, Tessa promised fervently. She wanted to be a winner more than anything else in the world. All the same, that mocking cry danced in her ears like a trapped echo long after Grant had vanished around the corner.

CHAPTER 2

Bright Street, the street Tessa lived on, ended in a small green lawn cut in half by the sidewalk. The council had put a garden seat there so that people could sit and watch the traffic go by, or stare at the tree . . . a shaggy-barked gum that looked like an umbrella turned inside out. When the tree was much younger, the council had cut out its center so that it would not grow too tall. Now its branches curved like grasping fingers springing from around a wide, blunt scar. It was under this tree that Tessa and Pete had erected the stand.

Directly opposite stood Sampson's Hamburger-ama and Fish-and-Chips Shop. To the left, on the other side of Bright Street, was a pet shop called Fish 'n' Cheeps. Next to Fish 'n' Cheeps was a small general store, Chilling's Superette, which sold milk and ice cream, pet food, frozen peas, and string—indeed, everything anyone might need suddenly during the weekend when all the other shops were closed.

Pete and Tessa spread their white elephant goods across a counter they had made from apple boxes, planks, and a small stepladder . . . homemade cookies, summer seedlings in old yogurt cartons, paperback detective stories with peeling spines, baby clothes donated by Tessa's older sister, Prue. On top of a carton sat a big monkey made of plastic, which was a money box as well as a toy. There was a slit in the top of the monkey's hat through which to drop your money. When you needed to count it, you simply unscrewed the monkey's head. Tessa would have preferred a real cashbox with a lock, but the Money Monkey would have to do.

Pete began arranging the bags of cookies, which he said he had made the night before. Tessa, however, knew his mother must have helped him.

While Pete lovingly set his cookies out in a straight line along the front of the counter, Tessa began to tack up the sign she had made on Wednesday night.

GOOD FORTUNES GANG WHITE ELEPHANT TELETHON STAND, it said. She thought TESSA'S TELETHON STAND would have sounded a lot neater, but, after all, she and her cousins were in this together.

A woman walking by paused to read the poster.

"You kind children," she said. "It's such a good cause, isn't it? We owe a lot to senior citizens."

Then she bought a bag of cookies.

"See? We've made money already!" cried Tessa as soon as the woman had gone. "And we haven't really begun yet."

Tessa dropped fifty cents through the slot in the top of the Money Monkey's hat. It echoed as it fell. Tessa tapped the figure 50 into the old adding machine and pulled the handle down. The paper roll jiggled and inched forward.

"You said we'd sell things for a dollar each," hissed Pete. "We'll never get a hundred dollars."

"This is just a beginning," Tessa said. "And I haven't even put up the picture yet. We're not official until the picture's up."

The picture Tessa had painted last night was one of the best she had ever done. It showed two rosy senior citizens waving small bags full of money and kicking up their heels with happiness. In between them danced a big white elephant playing music out of its trunk. Above the elephant's head floated a billowing cloud that was also a speech balloon. "Now you will be able to afford singing lessons *and* your knee operation," the elephant was saying in bright pink lettering. "Thanks to the Telethon you will be able to sing and dance forever and a day." Pete looked over Tessa's shoulder as she pinned up this picture.

"That elephant looks drunk," he said. "People might think that senior citizens will be spending the Telethon money on whiskey."

"It's happy," Tessa said indignantly. "They're having a great time." She loved her own picture. It had flowed out of her pens and paintbrushes as if it had been secretly waiting for the chance to get out onto paper. It wasn't often that a picture seemed to paint itself like that.

Grant Chilling shot by on his bike once more.

"Ha ha ha-*ha* ha!" he cried, like a motor horn. This time Tessa was really irritated with him. It wasn't fair. It just wasn't fair.

"Shut up!" she yelled, but he was already around the corner and heading off down Main Road, flitting off for the moment like a mosquito.

But it was only a few minutes before he came by again, bringing his only friend, Conrad Eddy, to buzz and sting with him.

Chilling and Eddy, thought Tessa. *This means trou-*

ble. She sighed. But Ellington Fillmore smiled from the back of the book cover. *In order to win, you must really want to be a winner,* he said.

And Tessa did want to be a winner. She wanted it more than anything else in the world.

CHAPTER
3

A woman came out of the Top Story Hair Salon and turned toward the stand under the tree. She wore high heels and carried a patchwork bag over one shoulder.

"A customer," hissed Pete.

"A client!" Tessa corrected him quickly. People in supermarkets were customers. *Client* sounded much more professional.

"Finky Fortune!" yelled Grant, but Tessa was too busy being professional to take any notice.

"Your hair looks great," she said admiringly as the woman went by. (Ellington Fillmore said you should find something nice to say to clients.)

"Nice try, kid!" said the woman, and laughed. But she stopped all the same, running her eye over the cookies, the shrunken baby clothes, and the vase.

"Oh, dear," said the woman. "I've got enough junk of my own already." But then she saw the candlestick shaped like a banana and began to laugh. "I'll take this," she said. "It's my sister's birthday next week. We always give one another crazy presents."

"A dollar," said Pete, pretending to look at the price.

"You must be joking!" said the woman. "It's expensive at fifty cents. I reckon I'm doing you a favor taking it off your hands, mate." She slapped a coin down on the counter. "Don't bother to wrap it."

Tessa sighed as the banana-shaped candlestick vanished into the patchwork bag and was carried off past Fish 'n' Cheeps.

"If we only get fifty cents for everything," she said, "we'll have to sell two hundred things. I don't think we've got that much stuff . . . I mean that much product."

Calling jars of plum jam and shrunken baby clothes *product* made her feel professional all over again.

Mrs. Meadowes, from the house next to Tessa's, came down Main Road and turned into Bright Street. She stopped, too, and bought a yogurt carton of cornflower plants. "I hope they're blue," she said. "Cornflowers ought to be blue. I'm not crazy about pink ones. And are those cookies hard?"

She poked at one cookie through the plastic bag and it crumbled a little.

"No," replied Tessa. "They're crisp."

"Oh, they're crisp!" cried a silly, squeaky voice. It was Grant, standing with Conrad one telegraph pole down Bright Street. Mrs. Meadowes pulled a face.

"My word," she said, "if I was that one's mother I'd have something to say to him." She took the cookies and cornflowers, paid two dollars, and went in through her gate, slamming it behind her.

"They're crisp! They're crisp!" yelled Grant. He and Conrad leapt onto their bikes again and began biking around and around the stand, swerving in closer and closer. They had really begun to annoy Tessa.

"Fortune cookies!" screamed Conrad. "Hey, Tessa, are you a Fortune cookie?"

"Get out!" she yelled, and turned to Pete. "Here comes another client. Get rid of Grant!"

"Me?" said Pete dubiously. But he ran at Grant and Conrad, who simply swerved away, laughing and jeering. Tessa could see that Pete had no chance of catching them.

CHAPTER
4

While two more clients were eyeing an ancient lamp, a shiny red Escort drew up beside the stand. Tessa recognized the car at once. In it were her aunt, Lorna Bancroft, and her cousin, Lorelei. Lorelei's father, Ivor, was the only person Tessa actually knew who had a cellular phone, but then he was the manager of the bank, and responsible for Tessa's own savings.

Lorelei scrambled out of the Escort and ran around to the back to open the trunk. She lifted out a box and, carrying it very carefully, brought it over to the stand. Inside was a beautiful cake, iced with soft, pale chocolate icing, piped with darker chocolate around the edges, and set with crystallized cherries and angelica.

"Gosh, it seems wrong to eat this cake," Tessa said, thinking it was beautiful enough to wear. The cake made everything else on the white elephant stand look shabby and old.

"Oh, dear!" said one client. "Just when I'm on a diet. Is this cake only a dollar?"

"Two dollars," said Pete quickly. Lolly, who was running back to the car, turned and made a face at them. Then she picked up another box, identical to the first.

"I'll take it," said the woman. "You'd pay ten dollars for a cake like this at Cream Castle," she added to her friend.

Cream Castle was the smartest bakery in Fairfield.

Lorelei set off to the car for the third time. She had brought three cakes with her, all equally beautiful.

"I'll collect you around about six o'clock," Aunt Lorna was shouting to Lorelei, waving and smiling from the driver's seat. The red Escort slid off, sounding as glossy as it looked.

"Did Auntie Lorna make these?" asked Pete, looking greedily at the cakes.

"No way!" said Lolly, waving as her mother vanished around the corner. "She makes good casseroles, but she's hopeless with cakes. She bought them for us from Cream Castle. They're her donation to the Telethon."

Tessa was shocked. She had sold a ten-dollar cake for two dollars. Not only that, the clients, after having a brief discussion on the other side of Bright Street, were coming back across the road.

"I'll buy one too," said the cakeless client, slapping two dollars down on the white tablecloth. Tessa was about to charge this client five dollars, when she caught the woman's beady stare and found she didn't quite have the courage to tell her that the price had suddenly gone up.

Conrad and Grant came biking past yet again. The sight of a customer paying money over the white tablecloth seemed to infuriate them.

"I wouldn't pay ten cents for your rotten stuff," Grant yelled. He saw a man coming down the Main Road sidewalk past Top Story. "Don't buy anything from them," he yelled. "Their dog peed on the cakes."

The man looked startled and kept to the far edge of the sidewalk, turning his head away from the white elephant stand. Tessa tried to reassure him.

"I haven't even *got* a dog," she called as he went by.

"Fresh cookies and cakes," cried Pete invitingly, but the man stared fixedly across Main Street at the Hamburgerama.

"Yaaaaah!" yelled Grant and Conrad triumphantly.

"He wouldn't have bought anything, anyway," said Lorelei. "He had a nonbuying face."

"Hey!" exclaimed Pete suddenly. He had picked up the foam tray that held cartons of cornflower plants and was staring into the box underneath it. "What did you bring these old tins for? They're empty."

There were fifteen small tins, and on each one there was a picture of a woman with a sun hat and an armful of yellow leaves. *Golden Haze Tobacco*, proclaimed the words on the top of each tin.

"I found them when I was cleaning out an old desk at the back of the empty shed at the grandys'," said Tessa. "Those tins were Great-Grandy Fortune's secret."

"The one with the geraniums on his grave," said Pete, who lived next to the old town cemetery and knew the names on the tombstones by heart.

"He was supposed to stop smoking," Tessa explained, "but he used to sneak into Grandpa Fortune's office and smoke there secretly. The bottom drawer of the desk had all these old tobacco tins hidden in it."

"He lived to be ninety-seven. It's on his gravestone," said Pete.

"If he hadn't smoked he'd have lived to be a hundred," said Tessa. "Or a hundred and ten!"

Conrad and Grant had propped their bikes against the Meadowes' hedge and came walking toward the stand with mincing steps, pretending to be real clients.

"Oh, look, a rubbish shop under the tree," said Grant. "You need rubber gloves and a gas mask to go shopping there. Stinky *old* stuff. Stink! Stink!" he yelled.

"Get out!" shrieked Tessa. "This stuff is for proper clients."

"I'm allowed to look at a stand on a public street!" said Grant. "You can't stop me!" He rattled money in his pockets.

A man and a woman came out of Fish 'n' Cheeps. They had two small white fluffy dogs on red leashes. The dogs ran with twinkling, rapid steps on paws that were almost invisible under their fluffy coats. It looked as if they were trundling along on wheels.

"I always go through secondhand books," the man said to the woman as they approached the stand. "I just might come across some treasure."

"The vase is cheap," said Lolly invitingly.

"It would need to be," said the woman, and laughed sarcastically.

Grant and Conrad, knowing they were safe, came right up to the counter, elbowing each other and giggling. They even jostled the man as he looked at the books.

"Hey, stop that," growled Pete.

"Yes! Stop that, Grant Chilling," cried Lorelei and Tessa in a scolding duet.

"Make me!" said Grant, stepping on one of the little dogs' paws. It began a piteous yelping. Both Pete and Tessa came around from behind the counter. The clients moved on hastily, taking their dogs with them, shooting angry glances over their shoulders. Conrad poked at one of the packets of cookies. Tessa tried to push his hand away. The bag of cookies fell to the ground.

"Ugh!" yelled Grant. "Throw them out. They've been on the ground."

"They're wrapped in plastic," said Tessa, brushing dirt off the bag.

"It doesn't matter," said Conrad. "If you try and sell them to anybody, I'll tell them those cookies have been lying on the ground."

Then he made a scooping gesture over the last of the Cream Castle cakes. He did not quite touch it, but he certainly threatened it. Tessa suddenly felt as if she were standing quite bare in a cold southerly wind, while being attacked by special cold-weather mosquitoes flying in much faster than she could slap them away. The stand, the cake, the books, and the cookies suddenly felt like a living part of Tessa, a part that needed protection.

Tessa ran at Grant, but he skipped away, and while she was chasing him, Conrad swept his arm across the counter, knocking the books all over the ground. Then Pete was on him, and they wrestled wildly, until Conrad brought his knee up hard into Pete's stomach. Pete sat down heavily. His mouth sagged open. He had a stunned look and made a whooping sound, as if he were struggling to get air into his lungs.

"Ha! Ha!" shrieked Grant, dancing away from Tessa.

"I'm the karate king!" yelled Conrad, dancing too, though he looked a little surprised at his own success. He had to shout because two heavy trucks were going by, swallowing all other noises with their roar.

"Fortune cookies! Fortune cookies!" yelled Grant.

Then he somehow zoomed around Tessa, and snatched up the vase.

"Hey, look at this!" he said, tossing it to Conrad, who caught it and threw it back. Lorelei dashed from behind the counter to help Pete stagger to his feet, looking as if he could not straighten up properly.

"Stop that!" Tessa cried as the vase flew through the air again. "That's an antique."

"Make me stop it!" Grant called triumphantly.

As he spoke he was grabbed from behind. It all took place so quickly that even Tessa did not quite see how it happened. She was as surprised as Grant, and he was horrified. He yelled and wriggled.

"She told you to *stop it*," someone said in his ear.

It was Tracey Fortune, fierce Tracey, and her brother, Jackson. The trucks going past had swallowed the noise of their approaching skateboard wheels. Grant had danced right back into Tracey's arms just as she had leapt off her skateboard, letting it run freely onto the grass. Now she threw her wiry arms around him and held him so tightly, he could not get away. She squeezed him, and then shook him from side to side, as if she were a terrier dealing with a rat.

CHAPTER 5

"Did you say *make me stop?*" asked Tracey. She was a tanned, tall girl with white-blond hair, and eyes so blue, they were startling in her sunburned face. Jackson, her younger brother of nine, stood beside her wearing black sunglasses that were a little too big for him.

"Let him go!" yelled Conrad. Though he was just as tall as Tracey, Tessa could see that Tracey alarmed him. Quickly passing the vase back to Lorelei, he turned to watch Tracey dealing with Grant.

"Listen, Eddy," Tracey said. "If you come one step closer, Chilling will really suffer. I'll bite his ear off."

Tracey's mouth looked dangerously close to Grant's ear.

"Keep away!" screamed Grant. Tessa was amazed

at his sudden fear. Ellington Fillmore had no useful advice about what an executive should do if one of the work force threatened to bite off a competitor's ear. Not only that, it was all too easy to imagine Mrs. Chilling erupting out of Chilling's Superette to protect her young.

"Don't hurt him, Trace!" Tessa cried anxiously.

"The last boy that said *make me stop* to a Fortune is a sad boy these days," said Tracey ominously. "He can't hear anything."

"No ears, man, no ears!" sang Jackson, strumming an imaginary guitar.

The strange thing was that Grant, who had seemed so tough a few moments ago, now looked small and pathetic, writhing in Tracey's grip.

"Were you interested in my cousin's white elephants, Chilling?" asked Tracey. "Help him, General Jackson!" She hooked one of her arms forcibly through Grant's. Jackson seized the other arm. Grant lurched a step forward. Tracey and Jackson hauled him back. He dragged behind, and they tugged him forward. Between them they hauled him over to the stand and stood him in front of the vase he had been so carelessly tossing around a moment earlier.

"Great vase!" cried Tracey enthusiastically. "Isn't it great, Chilling? Hey, your mother would love this for a present, wouldn't she?"

Grant struggled to unhook his arm from Tracey's.

"I know you like that vase," Tracey muttered into his ear.

Grant didn't say anything.

"Don't you?" she asked, nudging him.

"It's okay!" said Grant in a small, weak voice.

"Okay? That's not good enough. Say 'I think that vase is the prettiest thing I've seen all day,' " Tracey commanded him.

"I think that vase is very p-p-pretty," stuttered Grant obediently. Tessa saw with horror that he was really frightened. Conrad watched from a distance, alarmed and fascinated, like an antelope watching another antelope being devoured by a lion.

"I reckon Grant would like to *buy* that vase for his mother," said Tracey. "Don't you think he'd like to buy it, Jackson?"

"Sure do," said Jackson. "You and that vase go together, man, except the vase is way out prettier."

"Say 'I'd really like to buy that vase,' " Tracey said to Grant. He was silent. "Go on, say it!" she hissed in his ear.

"I'd like to b-b-buy . . ." Grant began. He was stammering again.

Tessa had forgotten that two years ago Grant had stuttered almost all the time. It wasn't fair. In spite of all Grant's teasing and tormenting she was beginning to feel sorry for him.

"Say it loudly," commanded Tracey, "so everyone can hear."

Grant was silent as he swallowed, trying to get his words in order. It must be terrible, thought Tessa, to be as frightened as Grant was. How had everything become so serious so suddenly? She looked up and down the street. A woman was hauling a complaining dog with a pointed nose into Fish 'n' Cheeps, but there wasn't a possible client in sight.

"Make him promise to leave us alone," Pete said to Tracey. He was breathing easily again. "Then let him go."

"Let him go?" Tracey cried indignantly. "He'd just ride off laughing at us. Go on, Chilling. Say 'I'd like to buy this vase.' "

"I'd like to b-b-buy this vase," stammered Grant.

"Right! Now *buy* it!" said Tracey.

Grant glanced timidly at Jackson's dark glasses, then felt in his pocket. He pulled out three coins . . . a dollar, a fifty-cent piece, and a five-cent piece.

"This vase is terribly cheap," said Tracey. "It's a dollar fifty."

"No, it isn't," said Tessa. "It's only twenty cents."

"You'll never make a hundred dollars," said Tracey, but she didn't argue. She seemed rather puzzled by Grant . . . someone who gave in so easily, someone who suddenly seemed to have thin, hollow bones like a bird. Tracey looked over at Conrad. "Hey, what sort of friend are you, anyway?" she asked scornfully.

"You said you'd bite his ear off," Conrad reminded her.

"Me? Bite his ear off?" Tracey cried. "I wouldn't bite *his* ear. Ugh! Yuck! I brushed my teeth this morning. Now, listen! If either of you gives my cousins a hard time I'll *get* you sooner or later. Because Jackson and I hear everything and go everywhere, don't we, Jackson?"

"Sure do, man! Here, there, and everywhere," said Jackson. His sunglasses slipped sideways.

Tracey let Grant go. He ran for his bike.

"Hey, Chilling!" called Tracey. Grant stopped as if he were on a leash and she had jerked him to a standstill. "You forgot your vase!"

Grant came back and took the vase from the counter. Tessa saw that tears were running down his cheeks. It couldn't have been from pain. Tracey had not actually hurt him. It might have been from fear but, after all, the worst was over. It occurred to Tessa that he might have been crying from a sort of shame. She looked over at Tracey, who smiled at her.

"Thanks for stopping him," Tessa said doubtfully.

Her thanks sounded faint and uncertain. Tracey's smile vanished.

"You *wanted* him to stop, didn't you?" asked Tracey.

"Yes," said Tessa "but I didn't want you to—to hurt his *feelings*." Tracey stared at her.

"Oh, terrific!" she said after a moment. "No hurt feelings! Right!"

Tessa felt that now, in some way she did not understand, she had actually hurt Tracey's feelings by not appreciating the protection Tracey had given her.

Tracey nudged Jackson.

"Come on, General," she said. "Let's split!"

"Right on!" Jackson said, straightening his sunglasses.

They set off together, going back up Main Road.

At the same time Tessa saw, coming down Main Road and about to cross Bright Street, a group of clients . . . three women, two of them with strollers.

Always see the positive side of new business opportunities, urged Ellington Fillmore.

"The show must go on," Tessa said, pushing things together so that the counter looked crowded again. Pete was gathering the books from the ground. The cake, luckily, had hardly been touched.

"Support the Telethon," Tessa called as the women came toward her. They stopped to browse and choose and smile, and slid a few coins into the Money Monkey.

CHAPTER 6

About fifteen minutes later Mrs. Chilling came marching out of Chilling's Superette, holding the vase in front of her by one of its china ears as if she could scarcely bear to touch it. She did not look at the stand under the tree, but crossed the road and vanished through Tessa's gateway.

"She looks mad, mad, mad," muttered Pete. "It's going to be bad, bad, bad."

Shortly after that Tessa heard her mother calling her. She turned around guiltily. Her mother and Mrs. Chilling were marching down Bright Street, side by side.

"Tessa," her mother said, sounding irritated and tired, "will you come here for a moment?"

"We'll watch the stand," murmured Lorelei.

Mrs. Chilling and Tessa's mother, Marama, met her halfway between the gate and the stand.

"Mrs. Chilling says that one of you grabbed Grant and forced him to buy this vase," Marama said angrily.

"I didn't," said Tessa.

"Apparently it was one of Peter Fortune's kids," said Mrs. Chilling. "The oldest one—that great big rough girl."

In a way it was a fair description of Tracey. But Tessa recalled Ellington Fillmore's instructions. *Support your sales force.*

"Tracey's only a little bit taller than Grant," she cried. "Anyhow, Grant and Conrad were jostling my clients. They knocked bags of cookies to the ground. And they grabbed that vase and threw it around."

Marama looked accusingly at Mrs. Chilling.

"A little bit of horseplay is quite different from deliberate bullying," Mrs. Chilling cried. "Grant's a very sensitive boy, and now he's in a fearful state. His money was taken from him. You Fortune kids ganged up on him. It was five against one. Ask Conrad Eddy!"

"No!" cried Tessa. "Truly, it wasn't." She looked at her mother, but her mother's expression was grim. "Grant and Conrad yelled at us, and called us names, and began to take our stuff, and Conrad hit Pete in the stomach and hurt him. No one hurt Grant. Tracey just grabbed him because he was being such a pain."

Mrs. Chilling took no notice of her. She looked at Marama instead.

"Five against one," she said. "All he wanted to do was to join in the fun. It wouldn't have hurt to ask him to help, would it? And now he's at the back of the shop, sobbing his heart out."

"It's not because he's hurt," Tessa said. "It's just that nobody likes him."

But this was the wrong thing to say. Mrs. Chilling looked furious.

"He's stuttering again. It was nasty bullying," she said to Marama. "I'm sorry. I want something done about it, or I'm getting in touch with someone—the school. Or the council!"

"Tessa," said Marama, "pack up your stand. It's causing too much trouble."

Tessa tried to recall every bit of good advice in Ellington Fillmore's book, but there was nothing to tell you what to do if your mother sided with the enemy and made you close your business down.

"But he knocked our cookies to the ground," she wailed. "And Conrad tried to stick his finger in our Cream Castle cake."

Both women suddenly looked impressed. Cakes from Cream Castle were not to be fingered by Conrad Eddy. Then Mrs. Chilling pulled herself together again.

"I can't be responsible for Conrad Eddy too," she said.

"Sorry, Tessa! At once!"

"Mom, it's for the Telethon. It's for a good cause."

"No," said her mother. "I know Tracey wouldn't hurt Grant, but she scared him badly. And he hasn't"—she paused—"he hasn't got anywhere else to play except around here."

"I have to work," said Mrs. Chilling, as if Marama had accused her of deserting Grant. "I'm not like some people who can spend all day at home if they want to."

"It's not fair!" Tessa cried, looking pleadingly at her mother.

"Maybe not," said Marama, "but the corner belongs to everyone, and neighbors are neighbors. I must say, Muriel," she said to Mrs. Chilling, "it sounds as if Grant was being a real nuisance."

"You Fortunes always stick together, right or wrong," said Mrs. Chilling. "Not all of us have a townful of relatives to back us up. And I want the money you stole from him too."

Tessa went back to the stand. She gave Mrs. Chilling twenty cents. Mrs. Chilling returned the vase in stony silence and marched back across the road.

"We have to stop," Tessa told Lolly and Pete. "We have to take everything inside again." Suddenly she knew she was going to cry. The work force should never see a manager break into tears, even if they happen to be cousins. Tilting her head back so that the tears could not run out of her eyes, Tessa pulled the poster and the picture of the dancing senior citizens away. But somehow the tears got into her nose. A sad wind blew down Main Road and spun around the corner. The Telethon poster rustled away down Bright Street, and the senior citizens poster, which was painted on cardboard, went cartwheeling, end over end, off on its own.

Pete and Lorelei folded the tablecloth in silence and then began packing up the planks. Tessa could feel their sympathy, but somehow it only made her disappointment worse. Salty tears started to drip out of her nose and run back into her throat, while possible clients, glancing curiously at the dismantling of the stand, went by.

Pete propped the ladder against the tree and rattled the Money Monkey. "Well, we've got something," he said comfortingly.

Suddenly, Grant appeared at the door of Chilling's Superette. He grabbed his bicycle, which was leaning beside the door, and cycled past them once more.

"Yaaahh!" he called triumphantly.

Tessa could not bear it. She wished that a cave would open at her feet. If it did, she would not hesitate to dive straight in, to live underground with worms and beetles forever.

Instead, she ran up the ladder and into the tree, scrambling into the big cup of branches. She climbed up along one branch, higher and higher, until she could see more sky than ground. There she sat, pretending there was no Telethon and no town, imagining herself to be the only person in a rustling, leafy world. She did not even think about the wisdom of Ellington Fillmore anymore. Nothing in his book, not even the words printed in capitals, could help a disappointed financial director forced to climb a tree to hide her tears.

CHAPTER 7

It was like being in a green room with all sorts of misshapen windows. Looking directly ahead Tessa found she could see straight down Main Road, which was growing busier as the day wore on. By evening there would be lots and lots of people outside the Hamburgerama opposite. And people would be going to Chilling's Superette because they suddenly needed milk or catfood. This would have been a great time to collect money for the Telethon.

As she watched, a horse and cart came down the road. The cart was decorated with streamers, and the driver wore a wig and a mask. PONY CLUB'S COLLECTION FOR THE TELETHON, read a splashy notice on its side. Girls in hard hats and jodhpurs were jumping off the cart and rattling boxes invitingly at passersby. *Those people giving money could have been* my *clients*, thought Tessa bitterly.

Below, she heard footsteps on Bright Street. Pete had taken two of the cartons into Tessa's house. Now he was coming back, and Marama was with him.

"Tessa!" she called from the foot of the tree. "Come on down, dear. We'll be making a contribution from the firm, and you can take it in if you like."

"*I* wanted to raise the money," Tessa cried back. "I wanted us kids to do it ourselves."

"I always feel so sorry for that wretched Grant," Marama explained. "Tracey can be rough at times."

"She just sort of stood over him, and talked at him," said Pete. "She didn't hurt him."

At that moment Grant went by on his bike again.

"Ha ha ha-*ha* ha!" he called rudely, and then, suddenly seeing Tessa's mother, he put his head down and biked off fast.

"See?" cried Lolly and Pete together.

"Oh, dear," said Tessa's mother. "It's so hard to be *fair*. Come on down, Tessa. I'll make a little treat for dinner . . . a cake or something."

"I want my *stand*, not a *cake*!" Tessa cried. "I've got a cake already, a cake from Cream Castle."

"I can't beat that," said Marama, laughing but

sounding a little sad too. "Oh, well . . ." She turned, and Tessa, looking down between leaves and twigs, watched her mother walk back down the road and through her own gate once more.

"Well, what's going on here?" someone asked. It was Mr. Martello, unusually spick and span, walking home with his hair and mustache freshly trimmed.

"Given up on the retail trade? What are you up to now? Oh, well . . . better not ask. As long as it's a good cause." Tessa heard the sound of a coin falling on top of other coins already in the Money Monkey.

The sound of falling coins had an odd effect on Tessa. She felt a little electric thrill pass through her. She scrambled down into the center of the tree and peered through the shaggy, cupped branches at Mr. Martello.

"It's a new plan," she said airily. "I'm staying up in the tree for twenty-four hours. People can sponsor me or give a donation."

The words came out as naturally and carelessly as if she had been planning them for hours.

"You? Sit up all night in the tree?" exclaimed Mr. Martello. "I'll pay you a dollar for every hour you stay there. How about that?"

"Done!" cried Tessa.

"It's a bargain," said Mr. Martello. "Get your lawyer to call mine."

As he went down Bright Street, Tessa could hear him laughing to himself.

If your strategy is not working, be prepared to change it, Ellington Fillmore had said in Chapter Three of his book. Tessa had just changed her strategy.

"Fetch me some cardboard, a notebook, and my felt pens," Tessa commanded her work force. "I'm going to do a tree-athon poster. And we need a book for sponsors to write their names and addresses in."

CHAPTER
8

TREE-ATHON, said the new poster. TESSA FORTUNE IS STAYING IN THE TREE FOR TWENTY-FOUR HOURS. SPONSOR THE TREE-ATHON, OR MAKE A DONATION TO THE TELETHON.

Pete nailed the new poster to the shaggy trunk of the gum tree.

"I'm her manager," he said to passersby. "I collect the money." He rattled the Money Monkey to prove it.

One woman laughed and made a donation.

"How much?" Tessa called down.

"Only twenty cents," said Pete. "We're back to our pre-Chilling total, plus whatever Mr. Martello just dropped in."

"Pass me up the adding machine," commanded Tessa.

There was a whir of wheels far down the road. Two familiar figures came speeding toward the corner. Two skateboards stopped suddenly, spinning on their back wheels.

Pete and Lorelei both began talking at once, telling Tracey and Jackson what had been happening.

". . . Mrs. Chilling came over to see Aunty Marama. . . .

". . . we had to give back the money you made Grant give us. . . ."

Tracey pulled a fearsome face.

"Grant Chilling will meet his doom," she said ominously.

"Forget him," Tessa said. "We've started a tree-athon. It's working out better."

"Will people pay just to see you sit in a tree?" asked Jackson. "I wouldn't."

"He hasn't got any money anyway!" Tracey said with a snort. "But you could sing or do something. Don't just *sit* there."

Tessa felt that faint electric thrill again.

"Pass me up one of the planks," she said. "I'll make a shelf for the adding machine."

A man in a smart tweed jacket with leather patches on the elbows stopped to look at the remains of the white elephant stall. He didn't look twice at the jam or the Cream Castle cake, but the lamp interested him for a moment.

A couple of women strolled up, and Jackson called to them.

"See that girl in the tree?" he cried. "She's going to sit up there all night to raise money for the Telethon."

The two women stared up at Tessa. The man put the lamp down, glanced at the vase, then looked away hastily.

"It's not safe," said one of the women.

"We'll be guarding her," said Tracey. "Jackson and me. We're getting our pup tent and sleeping under the tree."

"I am too," said Pete. "Would you like to sponsor her at twenty cents an hour?"

"Well, you've got to admit that they're trying," said the woman, grinning a little. She wrote her name and address in the sponsorship notebook. Twenty cents an hour.

"I'll bet the Telethon never sees a cent of that money," the cousins heard the other woman say as they walked away.

"Will Mom let us sleep out here all night?" Jackson asked Tracey.

"We'll ask in a *cunning* way," Tracey said.

As her cousins argued at the foot of the tree, Tessa began setting up an office among the branches.

"A *branch* office," she said, and smiled to herself.

Two old ladies came by, fresh from the Top Story Hair Salon, their hair looking very white and fluffy and smelling strongly of hairspray. They, too, stopped to read the new poster nailed to the tree.

"What will they think of next?" exclaimed the taller of the two, looking up at Tessa and laughing.

"What?" yelled the other old lady.

"The little children are helping the Telethon, dear," yelled the first old lady, pointing at Tracey, who was taller than she was.

"What?" yelled the second one, fiddling with her hearing aid.

"She's doing it for the Telethon, man," yelled Jackson, rattling the Money Monkey rhythmically in her direction.

The first old lady popped a dollar coin into the Money Monkey. The second one stared in astonishment at the Money Monkey being rattled in front of her. Then, opening her bag, she did the same. Other pedestrians stopped, too, wondering what was going on.

Tessa jammed boards between two branches to make shelves. She put the adding machine and the old desk calendar side by side, and suddenly she felt she really did have an office, even if it was up in a tree.

"Where did you get these?" asked the man in the tweed jacket, suddenly. He had come across the carton of old tobacco tins.

"They were hidden in the bottom drawer of my grandfather's desk," Pete said. "My great-grandfather hid them there. The poor old joker was a secret smoker."

No one was listening to his rhyme, so he had to laugh at it himself.

But Tracey and Jackson were impatient to be gone. They seized their skateboards. Off they went, sliding across Bright Street, going home to collect their pup tent.

"My own grandfather used to smoke this brand," said the man, rattling one of the tobacco tins curiously. "Suppose I give you . . . let me see . . ."

"Take them," said Tessa grandly.

"Oh, thank you!" said the man. "And let me give you a donation to the Telethon," and he pushed not a coin but a five-dollar bill into the Money Monkey, which was sitting on one of the apple boxes where

Jackson had left it. Then he picked up the whole carton of empty tobacco tins and set off down the road, carrying it under his arm.

"How much money have we got so far?" asked Lorelei.

"Fifteen dollars," said Tessa. Her heart sank. If she sat in the tree all night . . . sat there for another twenty hours, say . . . and Mr. Martello *did* pay the sponsorship money, which he had promised (partly because he thought Tessa would not last more than an hour or two up in the tree), that would mean thirty-five dollars. The hundred-dollar goal seemed to be getting farther and farther away. *Always remember that wise old saying, "When the going gets tough, the tough get going,"* Ellington Fillmore had said somewhere in his book. But Ellington Fillmore had not had to sleep in a tree all night.

As evening fell, Tracey and Jackson came skateboarding back again, and the smell of frying fish and hamburgers filled the air. Hungry people came to the Hamburgerama, and some of them crossed the road to see what was going on, just as Tessa had imagined they would.

"She's going to sleep up there all night," Tracey said over and over again, "and we're her bodyguards. Pull that rope tighter, Jackson."

They were busily putting their pup tent up under the tree. It was a small brown tent with a lumberjack painted on one side.

A cheerful, round-faced woman stared hard at Tessa.

"She can't really sleep there," she said, sounding dismayed.

"She'll have a sleeping bag," said Pete.

"Good luck, dear," said a man with sticking-out ears. "Rather you than me!"

Tessa leaned down out of the tree.

"If you think I won't be able to stay here, then sponsor me," she suggested. "It won't cost you much, and it's for a good cause."

"It's not an official event, is it?" asked the first woman.

"It's still on behalf of the Telethon," said Tracey.

"Well, anyone could *say* that," muttered the man with sticking-out ears, walking off in the direction of the Hamburgerama.

"Hey, we could have a barbecue here, and then people wouldn't have to go hamburgerama-ering," Tracey suggested.

"A barbecue!" exclaimed a deeper voice. It was Tessa's father, Findlay, suddenly appearing in the small crowd. "Tracey, don't tell me your parents have given you permission to camp out all night on a street corner?" he exclaimed.

"They have, Uncle Findlay. We asked Mom," cried Jackson quickly.

"I'll bet you rushed in while she was changing the baby and said you were coming around to our place to camp out with Tessa," said Findlay. Other members of the Fortune family were used to Tracey's cunning ways.

"Well, sort of," Tracey admitted. "But Mom is really grateful when we go out. Our house is too small for six kids."

A familiar truck turned off Main Road and into Bright Street.

"Uh-*oh*!" murmured Pete. This time it was *his* father, Toby, coming to collect him.

"Trace, your mom and dad won't want you sleeping out on a street corner. And I'm not going to let Tessa sleep up in a tree, so you can just forget all this."

"Dad!" wailed Tessa. "I have to. I'm being sponsored. People have paid money. I have to stay up here for twenty-four hours . . . for twenty-one hours, now."

"She's decorated the tree," said Pete.

Tessa gave him an angry look. This was not a

decorated tree. This was a tree with an office in it. Some of the crowd listened with interest. One of them took the sponsorship book from Pete and wrote in an offer, no doubt thinking that Tessa's time in the tree was going to be very short indeed.

"Dad, this is my branch office," Tessa said. An idea occurred to her. "It's a high-rise branch office."

Her father patted the stepladder.

"I suppose this is the ladder of success," he said, and the passersby laughed. "You can stay up there a little longer, but you can't sleep there. That's that."

"Can she stay up there until midnight?" asked Jackson. "Then she can sneak down, go to bed, and get back into the tree early in the morning. No one will know."

"I've promised not to," said Tessa.

"Yes, you *creep*, Jackson," said Tracey. "A Fortune always keeps a promise."

"*You* don't," said Jackson. "You promised me you'd give me that silver Frisbee when I turned nine, and then you didn't."

Tracey sighed deeply and shook her head as if Jackson had said something too silly to be worth any sort of explanation.

Uncle Toby had left his truck parked outside Tessa's house.

"What's happening?" he called as he cantered toward them.

"Tessa wants to sleep in a tree," said Findlay, "and I'm telling her she can't."

At that very moment the sound of music filled the air.

A white van came sailing down Main Road with its windows down and its radio playing loudly. It passed the Bright Street intersection, then slowed down and drew in beside Chilling's Superette. But once the driver had made sure that the street was clear behind him, it backed into Bright Street, parked, and stopped. TELETHON, Tessa read in giant letters along its side. It made her feel as good as one of Ellington Fillmore's sayings.

A man and a woman got out of the van, and most people under the tree recognized the man at once. His name was Harry Driver, and each night of the week he read the news on television. Just in time, thought Tessa. Like the hero in a story!

CHAPTER 9

"Did I see the word *Telethon?*" asked Harry Driver as he came up to the tree. "What's going on here?"

"It's a tree-athon!" cried Jackson, Tracey, Lorelei, and Pete, almost together. "She's staying up there all night."

Harry Driver read the poster. Then he walked right up to the tree and peered curiously at Tessa.

"Is this your idea?" he asked her.

"I am a branch vice-president, and I've set up my office in the tree," she declared quickly. "It's a high-rise branch office. I climbed the ladder of success. People are sponsoring me for the Telethon."

Jackson shook the Money Monkey wildly, doing one of his strange dances.

"She's really Tessa Fortune," said Tracey. "Jackson and I are her bodyguards."

Two other men had scrambled out of the van and were walking toward them. One of them was actually carrying a television camera.

"What do you think, Jock?" asked the first man. "General human interest stuff—straight off the street? They might use it."

"There's not enough light," one of the newcomers said.

"We got lights in the van. We could run a lead into the hair salon back there," the other one replied.

"Do you want to be on television, kids?" asked Mr. Driver. "Of course you do. Everyone wants to be on TV. I'm Harry Driver, slaving away out here on the fringes of civilization for the National Telethon. And this lovely lady is Stephanie, floor manager and chauffeur. You kids are all in on this together, are you? All your own idea, is it?"

As he talked, Tessa could see one of his helpers going down Main Road to the Top Story Hair Salon, dragging a length of black cable behind him like a tail. The woman and the third man were unloading lights from the back of the van.

"We started off having a roadside stand," said

Tracey, as if she had been in charge from the very beginning. Findlay and Toby had stepped back and stood silently watching.

"It was all Tessa's idea," said Pete.

People at the doors of the Hamburgerama paused to stare over at the tree-athon. Some of them even stopped playing on the video machine inside and came out onto the sidewalk. Tessa could see that they thought anything worth the attention of television must be worth their attention too.

"We are supporting the Telethon," Tessa cried. "We want to help old people and raise some money." *Seize the moment,* Ellington Fillmore had said. Tessa seized it. She began reciting the speech she had planned to give later as she delivered one hundred dollars into grateful hands at the Fairfield Telethon center. She found she knew it by heart.

Suddenly she was bathed in light from below. "Everyone should support the Telethon because we've all got grandparents, and anyhow, we're all going to be senior citizens ourselves one day," she ended.

"Great!" said Harry Driver. "Can you say that all over again in just a moment?"

"She can say it better next time," said Tracey, smiling proudly at Tessa.

"Silly question!" said Harry Driver, hitting himself lightly on the forehead. "Of course she can."

"I'll cue you in, Harry," said the young woman. "Don't you watch me, dear. This is just for Harry!"

Harry Driver began talking as if there were someone he had to impress only a few feet in front of him. His expression suddenly became serious, yet kindly. His voice deepened slightly.

"Telethon action isn't confined to the big cities and the big names," said Harry Driver. "Here's a local heroine, Tessa Fortune, conducting her own tree-athon. What's a tree-athon? Well, Tessa is preparing to sleep in a tree all night simply to raise money to help the old folks of the community. Tessa, can you tell us how you came to take on this amazing challenge?"

Tessa ran through her speech again. Tracey was right. This time it sounded even more fluent and sincere than it had the first time around.

"Great work," said Harry Driver. "Who says the young people don't care?"

He turned suddenly to Toby and Findlay, who were listening in amazement.

"You're part of Tessa's support team, aren't you?"

Toby and Findlay looked at each other. Findlay sighed.

"You bet we are," Toby said. "It's a long time since we were Boy Scouts, but we haven't forgotten how to camp out, have we, Fin?"

By now a crowd had flocked over from the Hamburgerama, and lots of people were staring up into the tree. Some of them couldn't wait to start on their hamburgers, or fish and chips, and began eating them right there, staring at Tessa as if she were already on television. Others watched Stephanie and the rest of the crew pack their equipment and themselves back into the van. Many of these new clients dropped their change into the Money Monkey. One man actually gave ten dollars.

"Will I be on television?" Tessa asked Harry Driver as he helped wind up the last cable.

"Don't know!" he said. "There's a lot going on. Don't worry! We'll do our best to make a star of you."

"Shall we use my tent or yours?" Toby asked Findlay. "It looks like we'll both be camping out tonight."

"You're mad, do you know that?" said Findlay. "But why not? After all, it's for a good cause, isn't it?"

CHAPTER
10

By the time evening came, there were two tents on the grass under the gum tree. Tracey, Jackson, Lorelei, and Pete sat outside one of them. Findlay and Toby had put the other one up for themselves.

Tessa was far more comfortable than she had ever expected to be. Her father and Toby had hoisted an old narrow mattress between the brown fingers of the tree. Though it rather spoiled the look of the office, it would certainly provide a restful surface to sleep on.

"That's great!" Tessa had cried, perched above them, watching Findlay struggling to make it secure. "I won't be able to stretch myself out, though."

"You should have thought of that before you started all this," said Toby. "Move farther up. I need room."

He was climbing the ladder, pulling up after him something that looked like a blue fishing net. Tessa swarmed to the top of the tallest branch and looked out through the leaves at roof level.

Fish 'n' Cheeps was dark now, but light still spilled from Chilling's Superette. Grant stood on the Fish 'n' Cheeps corner watching the the tree-athon. He looked small and ghostly, shrunk by the evening light, and Tessa found herself wondering what it would be like to live in the back of a shop with parents who worked seven days a week from morning to night. Grant had a wonderful bicycle, but no cousins. His father would never put a mattress in a tree for him if ever he needed one.

"There! Try that!" called her own father, climbing back down the ladder. Tessa scrambled through a web of ropes. It was a a blue nylon hammock her father and Toby had rigged in the tree for her. It swung between two main branches. Guy ropes led off in all directions. She felt like an executive spider.

"Get into it carefully," her father warned her. "You've got to be tactful with hammocks."

At first it did feel dangerous, as if the hammock might dissolve or turn over sideways. Tessa lay extremely still, staring up into the leaves.

"If you fall out . . ." began Findlay.

Think positively, Ellington Fillmore would say.

"I know I won't fall," she said quickly.

"*If* you fall, the mattress will be under you," said Toby. "After that it's anyone's guess. But you won't fall," he added quickly. "That hammock has been put up by experts."

"We've all had lots of tree practice," said Tracey. "We have secret meetings in the tree behind the grandys' house."

"How's it going?" asked someone, and a chorus of voices answered, some of them Fortune voices and some of them the voices of curious clients, keen to give donations to the treeathon, and who consequently felt entitled to join in.

Lorelei's parents, Aunt Lorna and Uncle Ivor, walked up, arm in arm. They had driven over from the smart side of Fairfield to say good night to Lorelei, who was squeezing into the small tent with Pete, Tracey, and Jackson.

Although he was not a Fortune uncle, Tessa enjoyed Uncle Ivor's company because he did not make fun of her when she talked about investments. Nor did he tell her that money wasn't the most important thing in life. He climbed the stepladder and looked into the branch office.

"See my adding machine?" Tessa asked, pointing proudly to her shelf. "And my desk calendar?"

"I haven't seen an adding machine like that for years," said Ivor.

"We're going to make a hundred dollars," Tessa said. "So far we've got nearly fifty dollars . . . that's counting the twenty dollars that Mr. Martello will give me if I stay up here all night. He's sponsoring me at a dollar an hour, and I've been up here four and a half hours already."

"The Telethon's showing on television right now," said someone down below. "Tessa won't get a chance to see herself."

It was only then that Tessa understood she was going to miss seeing almost all the television part of the Telethon. She would be up here in the tree until sometime tomorrow. She was probably going to miss her own speech.

"Don't worry," Findlay said. "We'll load up the video. And remember, you can always change your mind and come down."

"No," Tessa said. She had set her goals. She was determined. All the same, suddenly there was something chilly about shop lights and streetlights—and the night beyond them.

Then Findlay and Toby left to have proper cooked dinners, saying they would be back later. Tessa's house was only a few yards away, but it felt spooky watching the grown-ups walk off.

Ivor opened the door of his car, which was parked behind Toby's truck. He climbed halfway into it, and then he hesitated. At last he came back to the tree, carrying something as if it were precious.

"You can borrow this," he said, handing that something up to Tessa. "Keep in touch!"

It was his cellular phone. Tessa stared at it—she couldn't believe her luck.

"You can dial any phone in town," he said "But you have to dial zero two eight first to get into the right network. Can you remember that?"

Tessa did not know what to say. The figures 028 blazed in her head. Just for a moment she couldn't help imagining herself punching in a number for New York. "Sell my shares and buy another lot," she would say to someone on the other end. "And put the profits into diamonds." But she had no reason to make long-distance calls, and no shares either.

"Thank you, thank you!" she called.

"Look after it," said Uncle Ivor. "And remember, it costs sixty cents a minute to make a call on a cellular phone."

The New York vision went out like a light.

Tracey, who had gone with Jackson to buy fish and chips, came back across the road.

"Maxie gave us the chips free," she said. "If we're on television again, we've got to mention his shop."

Outside Chilling's Superette, Grant lingered, looking more and more pathetic, like someone on a desert island watching a party on a faraway beach.

"Shall we let Grant have a few chips?" Pete suddenly suggested.

"Never!" cried Tracey. But Tessa felt full of kindness toward Grant. If it hadn't been for him she would not be here up in the tree with Uncle Ivor's cellular phone. She remembered his mother saying, *All he wanted to do was to join in the fun.*

"Ask him over," she said. "Tell him we forgive him."

"You're really weird, Tessa," said Tracey, but for once she did as she was told.

"Hey, Grant! How about some chips?" she called. "Come on over. I won't bite your ear off. I've got my own fish and chips now."

But Grant darted back into the shop as if her kind words were a sort of threat.

More likely clients came by and peered up at Tessa. Many laughed. A few frowned. As they approached, Jackson leapt up, dancing and holding out the Money Monkey. When they had walked past, Jackson would tell Tessa how much money he thought they had given. Then Tessa would enter the new sum on the old adding machine, pull the handle, and call out the new total to her cousins, who already knew what it must be. The adding machine simply made it official.

The evening gradually grew quiet. Cars going down Main Road sped past the Hamburgerama and Chilling's Superette without stopping. At the foot of the tree Tracey, Jackson, Pete, and Lorelei laughed and talked softly. Every now and then one of them would shout something up to Tessa. After a while she began to feel cut off, even lonely, particularly when they began to take turns going into Tessa's house to watch the Telethon on television.

"Have I been on yet?" she asked each returning cousin, but the answer every time was no.

Always remember, it is lonely at the top, Ellington Fillmore had said.

"I'm at the top," Tessa muttered to herself.

All over town images of television newscasters in funny hats, laughing and saying what great *generous* people New Zealanders were, would be flickering in most houses. And here she was, up a tree, with hours and hours and hours and hours to go before she could come down to earth again. For the first time in her life being up in a tree seemed a terrible ordeal. Tessa turned on the flashlight and looked at the cellular phone. She tapped in 028 and then her own phone number. Her sister, Prue, answered the phone.

"Prue, this is Tessa, up a gum tree," she said.

"How's it going?" asked Prue in a comfortable voice.

"Have I been on television yet?"

"Not yet . . . we're all waiting for it, though."

"What's the national total?"

"I don't know! About eighty thousand dollars, I think. But it's only just begun, and you know how they save the really huge amounts till the very last."

Tessa reckoned she had talked about sixy cents' worth of cellular phone time.

"I'm getting into my sleeping bag now," she said. "Good night!"

She wormed her way into the sleeping bag, then very carefully rolled herself into the hammock, which swayed and sagged alarmingly. Her bottom was only about half an inch above the mattress. As she settled down, the strangeness of the night, of being suspended in a tree, feeling like a spider in the middle of a web, swept over her. She clasped the phone to her heart.

A solitary possible client went by. Jackson leapt out, rattling the Money Monkey, and the man dropped in a coin. The lights went out, first in Chilling's Superette and then in the Hamburgerama. Tessa heard the Chilling car leaving for somewhere,

sounding loud and irritable. Sixteen hours to go. *Sixteen!* She wasn't even halfway through her tree-athon.

I'll never go to sleep, Tessa thought. *I'll be awake all night.* But she did go to sleep soon after. She hung in her hammock like a butterfly in its chrysalis, and did not hear her father and Toby scramble into their tent, half grumbling, half laughing as they did so. She floated in and out of sleep, swinging in the hammock up in the tree, the phone held over her heart. Sometimes her eyes opened and she looked up through the leaves and saw a star or two overhead. But she did not wake properly again until a milk truck went rattling by in the gray light of early morning, and the last day of the Telethon began.

CHAPTER
11

At three o'clock the following afternoon, when Tessa finally came down from the tree, she felt she was setting foot on an undiscovered planet. The Fortune family, including her grandparents, were there to welcome her, just as if she had been away for years, and not simply in her own high-rise branch office for twenty-hours. Mr. Martello was also there with a small crowd of neighbors and onlookers.

"Congratulations!" he said, and gave her a twenty-dollar bill. "I didn't expect to be paying out this much, I can tell you."

"You owe me an extra fifty cents," Tessa said. "I was up there for twenty and a half hours. I'd have stayed there longer, but I have to go to the studio now."

"You Fortunes are a tough bunch," said Mr. Martello as he gave her an extra fifty cents.

"Have I been on television yet?" asked Tessa. She had asked that question regularly all morning, as relatives came and went, but her interview with Harry Driver had not been shown.

Even though she had done what she had set out to do, Tessa had a curious floating feeling that was very like disappointment. She had not made a hundred dollars, yet she couldn't bear to sit in the tree another moment.

"We'll all chip in to bring the total up," said Uncle Peter, Tracey's father.

"It's wonderful to have you back on earth again," exclaimed her mother, and hugged her.

A sound of clapping reached Tessa's ears. Across Main Road, Mr. Sampson of the Hamburgerama was applauding her. On the other side of Bright Street, Grant Chilling and Conrad Eddy watched in silence.

"Let's take the money in now," said Tessa. "I want to get rid of it."

The Good Fortunes Gang crowded into the back of Toby's truck, drove to the Fairfield town hall, and joined the line of people waiting to pass in Telethon contributions.

Everyone in the line was friendly. People gossiped and compared notes. A woman in front of them had held a knit-athon. She had knitted cardigans for babies and had raised $275. A little girl of five had been sponsored to tidy her room and had earned four dollars.

Inside the hall a scattered audience was watching a local band play rather wearily. By evening the hall would be crowded again, and everyone would be watching the national total flash up on the big screen behind the stage, waiting to sing the Telethon theme song. Tessa had imagined herself being part of this crowd, but all she wanted now was to be at home, watching the television from her usual chair, with her father and mother and sister, Prue.

"And here's another contributor," cried one of the hostesses, swooping on Tessa. There were no television cameras. Indeed, there was almost no one watching this great moment.

"Is Harry Driver here?" Tessa asked.

"He's taking a coffee break, love!" said the hostess. "They've been on the go all night, and he's heading back to the city in a few minutes."

Tessa passed the Money Monkey over and tried to remember the speech she had made so well yesterday, but not a word of it came back to her. "This money is from the Good Fortunes Gang," she said at last. "It's a hundred dollars."

"Wonderful," cried the hostess. "That's amazing. A hundred dollars. And you earned it all yourselves?"

"We made eighty-three dollars sixty-three cents ourselves," Tessa said truthfully.

"Wonderful. Thank you all *so* much," said the hostess, and Tessa saw her eyes were already moving on to the next person in the line.

As the Good Fortunes Gang left the town hall and walked back to where the truck was waiting for them, someone suddenly called out:

"Hello there, Jungle Queen!" It was Harry Driver himself, making for his van in the parking lot.

"She stayed in the tree for twenty-four hours," cried Jackson, exaggerating only a little. "She did it, and we've just taken the money in."

"Eighty-three dollars sixty-three cents," said Tracey, "only our fathers had to add some to make it up to a hundred dollars."

"Great!" cried Harry Driver enthusiastically.

"I wanted to do it myself," said Tessa. "I wanted to be the one who raised a hundred dollars with my ideas. And I wanted to be on television."

"Look, I tried," said Harry. "But you're competing with Miss New Zealand, the prime minister, rock

stars . . . all the heavies! Just relax and go with the flow, kid. And have fun! That's partly what it's all about, you know. Fun!" Then he was gone.

Later that night, bathed and clean, Tessa sat between her parents, with Prue and the Fortune cousins around her, watching the last half hour of the Telethon on the television screen. The Telethon's wandering cameraman was out in the street where Cliff Harding, the anchor for the evening news, was standing on the back of a truck, auctioning various things that people had donated to raise money for this good cause.

"And then there's this!" he cried. "One of our vans brought it in from the Fairfield-Rangatiki area, where they're all so artistic. How's this for a memento of the Telethon!"

Tessa stared. There it was: *her* picture of the dancing senior citizens and the white elephant! Someone, perhaps Harry Driver himself, had picked it up in the streets of Fairfield. Someone had liked it and carried it all the way to the city and propped it up among the auction goods, just for fun. There was no doubt about it. It *was* her picture. The camera focused on it. Tessa could remember drawing every line of it. Yet, there on the screen in front of her, it looked better than she remembered it, and as remote as if it had been drawn by someone else. Her picture looked like art.

Someone bid two dollars for it. And then a man in a trendy suit bid twenty. Tessa's mouth fell open. So did her mother's.

"That's a generous bid," said Cliff Harding. "You must think it's a good cause, sir."

"I just like the picture," said the man. Cliff Harding went on to auction something else, but, as her family shouted and exclaimed around her, Tessa watched what was going on in the background. The man in the trendy suit paid the money and claimed her picture . . . his picture now . . . and then walked away with it. He moved out of focus. His figure blurred and vanished, and her picture vanished with him.

"You did make a hundred dollars, after all," said Tracey, looking at Tessa with a sort of puzzled respect.

"How *did* it happen?" cried Jackson. "It's like magic."

"Amazing things do happen," said Tessa's father. "Last night I was talking to a fellow I know . . . Jack Fern, who runs an antiques shop over in Rotorua, and apparently he had a real stroke of luck . . . picked up a lot of old tobacco tins dirt cheap."

"Who'd want old tobacco tins?" asked Tracey.

"People collect them. And these were good ones," said Uncle Peter. "Fifteen old tobacco tins in mint condition . . . not dented, not rusty. He reckons he'll get twelve dollars apiece for them. That's a hundred and eight dollars picked up off the side of the road. Now, how's that for good luck?"

Yaaaaah! cried a voice in Tessa's head. It was just as if the ghost of Grant Chilling on a ghostly bicycle were riding through her thoughts. The world around her shivered.

But she took a deep breath and smiled. Suddenly she felt she understood something she had not understood before. Even with a whole bookful of good advice from Ellington Fillmore, the world of an executive vice-president was just like a fairy tale after all. Sometimes you had good luck, and sometimes you had bad luck. Tessa flopped back in her chair, and right then she began to think about the possibility of being a famous artist instead of an executive vice-president. After all, she had already sold a picture, even if it was by accident, and if she had taken the first step on the ladder of success, shouldn't she keep going until she got to the top?

ABOUT THE AUTHOR

Margaret Mahy is an internationally acclaimed storyteller who has twice won the British Library Association's Carnegie Medal and has received the (London) *Observer* Teenage Fiction Award. She has also won the Esther Glen Award of the New Zealand Library Association five times. Of her teenage novels published in the United States, *The Changeover* was a Best Book of the American Library Association and was the International Board on Books for Young People Honor Book in 1986. *Memory* was a *School Library Journal* Best Book and a *Boston Globe/Horn Book* Honor Book. She has written more than fifty books for young readers.

The exuberant adventures of the extended Fortune clan began with *The Good Fortunes Gang*, and *A Fortunate Name*, books one and two of the Cousins Quartet.